LUCKY
needs help

This book belongs to

....

....

Vision Street Publishing Llc.
2900 Glades Circle, Suite 850
Weston, Florida, C.P. 33327
USA
www.visionstreetpub.com
Tel.: +1(954) 626 3789

Author and Editor:
Dilpreet Kaur and Rennie Thomas

This edition is published in 2019
Printed in India, March 2019
First edition.

Sammy the puppy has been adopted and now lives in a new home. It's a big house where he can run and play with his favorite ball.

Lucky also lives in the same house. Lucky is a cat. She doesn't want to play with Sammy. She finds him too noisy and too busy. She likes it when it's quiet in the house.

While Lucky is lying on the couch in the living room napping, Sammy bursts out loudly from the kitchen running after his ball.

Lucky looks up angry and leaves the living room. She goes into the kitchen.

Lucky jumps on the counter and sees kitchen towels nicely folded inside. They smell fresh from the laundry.

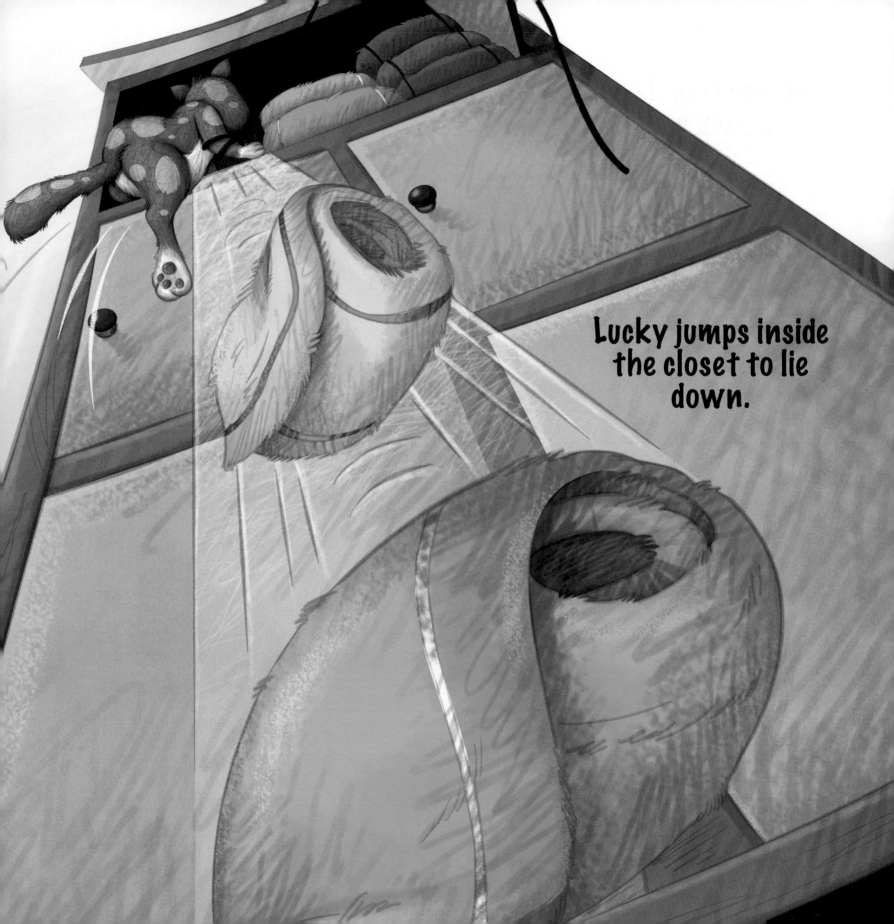

Lucky jumps inside the closet to lie down.

But the moment she lands on the towels, the door closes behind her.

The towels are soft like Lucky expected, but it's dark in the closet.

Lucky starts to meow.
Maybe Sammy will hear her
and help her.

But Sammy is busy playing in the living room. He's running after the ball and doesn't hear Lucky.

Lucky starts to meow harder.
At that moment, Sammy's ball
rolls towards the kitchen.

Lucky meows one more time. Sammy approaches the closet where the string is hanging.

He grabs the string with his teeth and pulls. The closet's door starts to move.

He pulls harder and the door finally opens.

Meow, Meow.

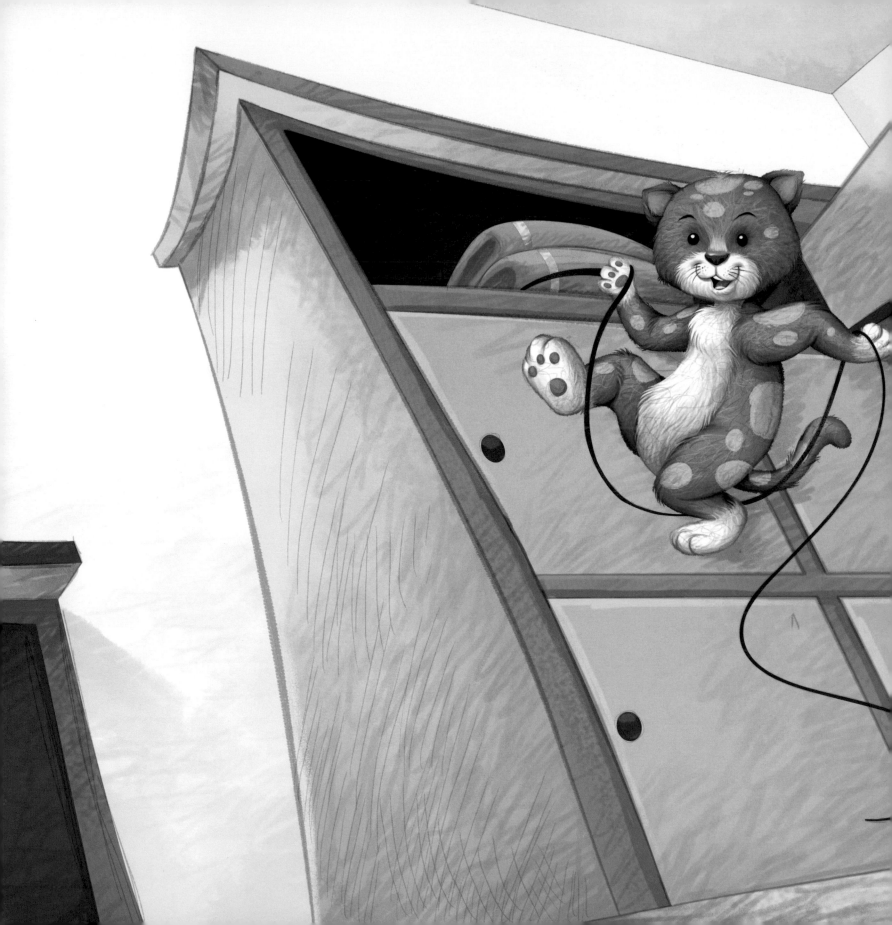

Lucky was very excited when the door opened. She started to climb down the cupboard while Sammy eagerly waited for her.

Lucky jumps out.
"Thank you! Thank you!"
"You are welcome" says
Sammy.

"How did you get in the closet?" Lucky starts explaining the story to Sammy.

Lucky looks at the ball and asks shyly
"Can I play with you?""Of course!"
answers Sammy excited!

Sammy and Lucky play
the rest of the afternoon
together with the ball.

From then onwards, Sammy and Lucky play everyday together, except when Lucky wants to take a nap.

Playing with a friend is always more fun than playing alone, but you also have to respect when someone wants to rest.